# the BIG
## and the small

**A SOUL STORY**

Jane
Brunette

flaming seed
press

*ISBN 978-0-9892605-4-1*

*Book design and scribbles: Jane Brunette*

FLAMINGSEED PRESS
*flamingseedpress.com*

This book emerged from the methods of writing-as-meditation that I share through Writing from the Soul. Please use it as inspiration to make a book from your own soul story. Visit the website for resources to access the truth, guidance and creative juice hidden inside each one of us.

*—Jane Brunette*
writingfromthesoul.net

*for all who sense that there is*

*more to being human than what*

*the advertisers preach and*

*search for an opening to a self*

*which is vast and intimate,*

*ancient and new:*

*Please don't ever give up.*

# Once upon a time

there was a very small girl

living in a very small house

in a very small world.

# She was sitting in the backyard of the very small house

under a very small apple tree and saw

*a golden candy* sitting on a silver platter

inside a deep knot in the tree's trunk.

It reminded her of the golden coin

chocolates of her childhood,

so she popped it into her mouth

and swallowed it.

As it went down
her throat,
it tasted not at all
like chocolate

but like red wine and fire,

turkish coffee, elixer,

and the pungent, dark medicine
of a shaman.

# She tried to cough it up, but it was too late.

The little golden candy was inside her now.

It broke open and released

a great **power?**

At first, she thought
the power was
just a digestion problem.

But when she got up

and walked toward

her very small house,

her body felt

immense.

She looked at her reflection

in the very small window

of her very small house

and saw that she had not

changed sizes at all,

and everything around her

seemed just as it was before.

.

Still, everything felt

way too tiny for her size.

How confusing.
She was small.

There was no getting around it.

Her smallness was a fact.

She still fit in her very small bed.

She still ate her very small food.

She still lived in her very small house

and wore her very small shoes.

And yet inside, she was

enormous.

At first she thought that it could be a digestion problem.

But as she got up and started walking toward her very small house, her body felt immense. She looked at her reflection in the very small window of her very small house and saw that she had not changed size. It was only that she had not changed size. It was only that everything about her seemed just too big. Everything felt way too tiny for her size.

"How could I possibly be BIG and small at the same time?"

she wondered.

As the days went by, this feeling got more and more uncomfortable.

It always felt as though

her clothes were too small,

but when she looked in the mirror,

they were fine.

Then one day, she had the thought

that maybe her skin was too small

and this frightened her.

There was nothing she could do about

the size of her skin. But the self inside felt

**bigger than her body
could hold.**

# finally,

she decided she had to leave

her very small house and search

for a larger world

where she would fit better.

And so she filled her

very small backpack

with her very small clothes

and some very small snacks,

and she walked out of the gate

of her very small house and traveled to

# the very large world.

# At first, it was a relief to be there.

It seemed that all the very large things

were just right for how she felt

and she walked around freely,

finally able to move

without the feeling of constriction.

Soon, she grew thirsty,

but when she went to get

a drink of water,

she couldn't lift the glass.

And then an

## enormous

### person walked through

and nearly stepped on her,

like a little bug.

"I've got to get out of here," she thought.

So she ran back to her
very small world, but it was gone.

In her absence, wild fires had come

and destroyed her village.

The smoke was hovering over the town

she thought she'd go to instead

and it made her choke.

Then she heard of a very small cabin

on a very small mountain

but by the time she got to the crossroads

that would take her there,

a bird brought her a message:

the fire had gone there too

and they had to evacuate.

She could not stay

in the very small cabin.

So she could not return to her very small world.

But she could not live in the very large world

because her body was too small for it and

she would be crushed. **And so she wandered,**

looking for very small crevices

in the very large world where

she could stay and feel safe.

But she was a refugee now

and longed to find a home.

One morning, she got up determined
to resolve this once and for all.

She left the very large world and roamed through

the forest, looking for the place where you could

be big and small at the same time, but she wandered

the whole day and found nowhere in particular.

Twilight was coming and so was the cold.

Again, she was looking for a soft place to sleep,

just another crevice to protect her from the wind,

and she yelled out in frustration,

"Won't someone please tell me
where a person who is
big and small at the same time
ought to live?"

And she crawled into a crevice

between the rocks to sleep.

# When she woke up,

she saw two eyes looking at

her in the darkness,

a light shining off them.

# "Who are you?"
she asked.

The eyes didn't answer.

They just watched and saw her —

seemed to see everything about her.

They were steady, warm, loving, present,

and she breathed out

a sigh of relief.

"**I** hope you can answer a question for me," she said to the eyes.

"Where does a person who is big and small

at the same time go to live?

The big world is too big

and the small world is too small."

The eyes blinked once and watched,

steady, warm, loving, present.

"When you are big and small at the same time,

you are very lucky. You can live anywhere,"

the eyes seemed to say.

"No, you don't
            understand,"
                        she said.

"When I am in a small place,

I feel too big for it.

And when I am in a big place,

I feel too small for it."

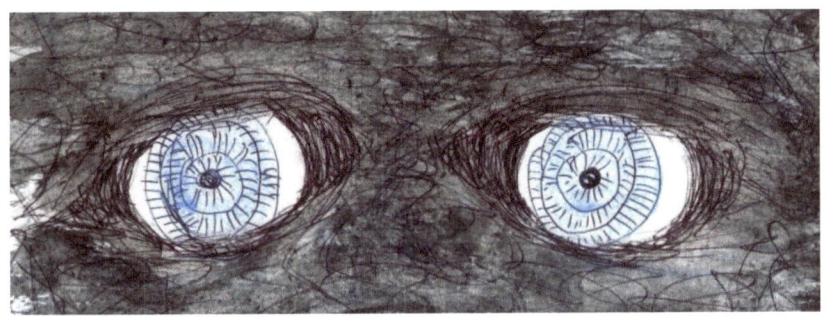

# "Then you are not big and small at the same time yet,"

the eyes seemed to say.

"You are one and then the other,

and lucky for you, they are not matching

the place you are in."

"How could that possibly be lucky?" she asked.

"It is terribly uncomfortable."

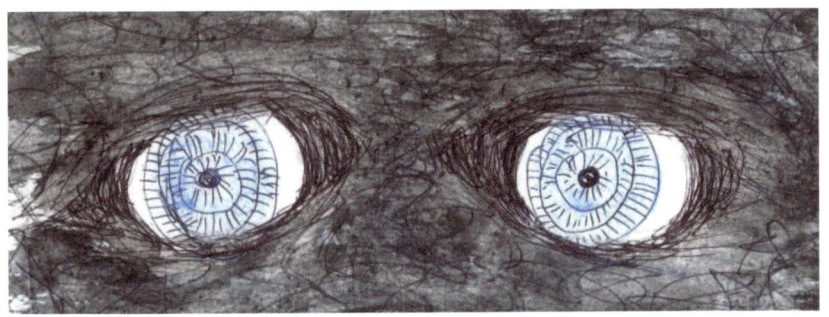

"Yes, and that is the good news,

    for if you were small in small places,

    you would think you were only small

    and never know that you are also big.

        If you were big in big places,

        you would think you were only big

        and then you would unthinkingly

        crush anything small.

    So lucky for you,

    you don't make this mistake

    because you have the discomfort

    of knowing the truth."

"But then
where can a person
like me go to live?

It is so uncomfortable,

to stay as I am.

Everyone else seems

to pick one world

and just live their life,

but I can't pick a world

because none of them fit."

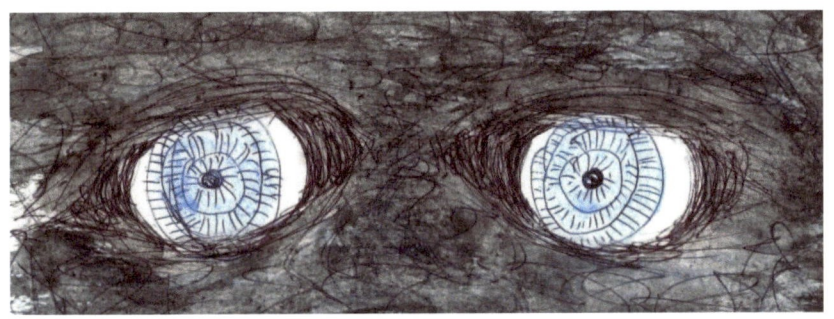

# "You already know the answer,"

the eyes seemed to say.

"You said it before."

## "What did I say?"

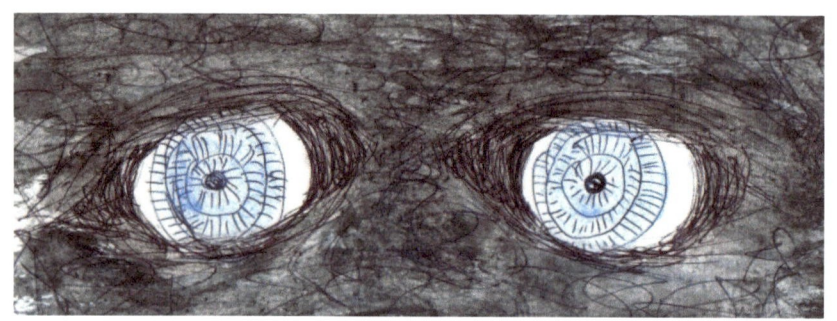

"You must be
BIG
and small
at the same time."

# "You are no help at all,"
## the girl said,

and the pain of exile filled her whole being

and she cried until she could cry no more.

**Finally,** she felt soft and spent.

She put her hand on her own heart.

Her body felt tender, relaxed,

and she felt strong again.

When she looked up,

the eyes were still there—

steady, loving, present.

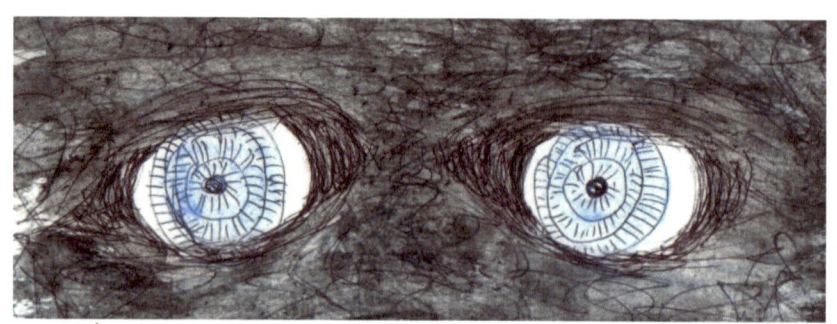

"Are you

BIG

or are you

small

right now?"

the eyes seemed to ask.

The girl felt her strength

and she felt her tenderness,

and they were both there together.

"I guess right now
I am big and small
at the same time,"
she said.

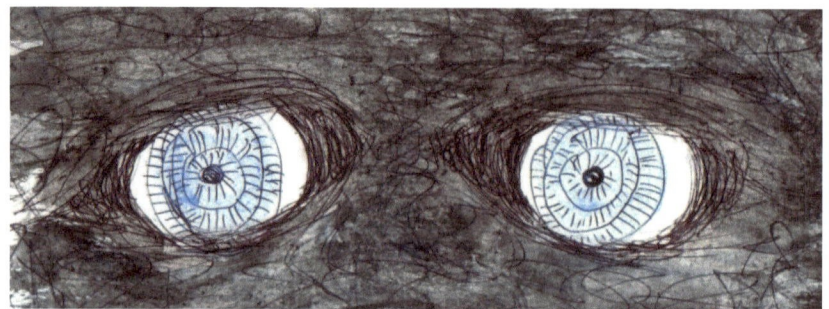

# "Well then, the problem is solved.

Stay like that and you can live anywhere.

In the small world,

you will remind others of their bigness

and they will not be afraid of being crushed

when their world burns down.

In the big world,

you will remind others of their smallness,

and they will remember to look underfoot

when they walk, and to leave little sweet spaces

for the small beings to rest.

The only problem you will encounter

is if you pretend that you are one or the other

because now that is impossible.

You can never be just small or just big

and hide out and relax in one world or the other

with all the others who are asleep to their wholeness.

Like it or not, you will always be big and small

at the same time, and once you know it,

there is no going back.

This is your power
and your medicine
for the world."

"Will you
come with me,
then,
to remind me?"
asked the girl.

"I have always been with you,"

the eyes seemed to say.

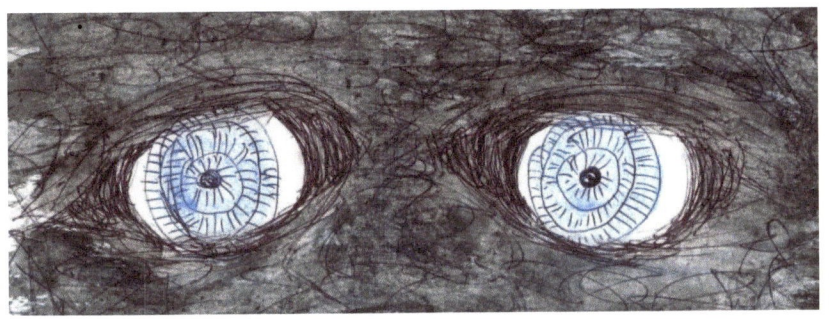

"I am the eyes
of your
bigness."

# And so

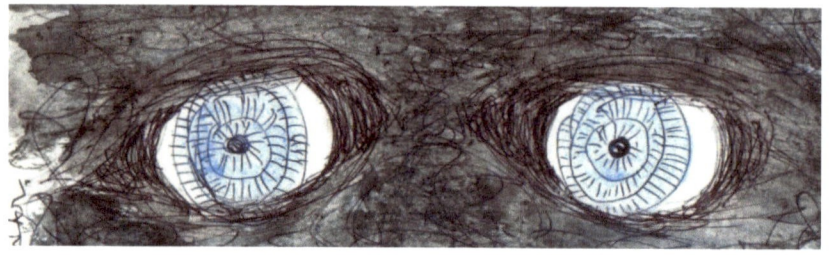

the next day,

the girl went to the

## big world

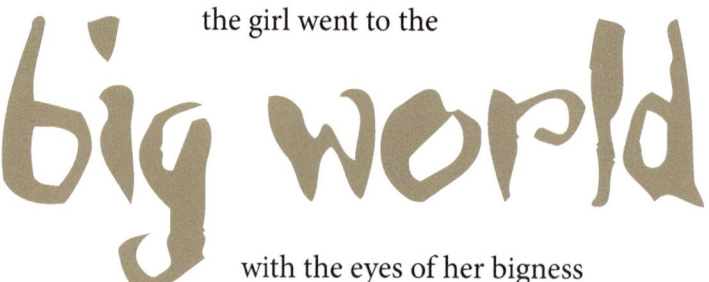

with the eyes of her bigness

and held the small one close and safe,

able to dodge the crushing feet

with her wide seeing.

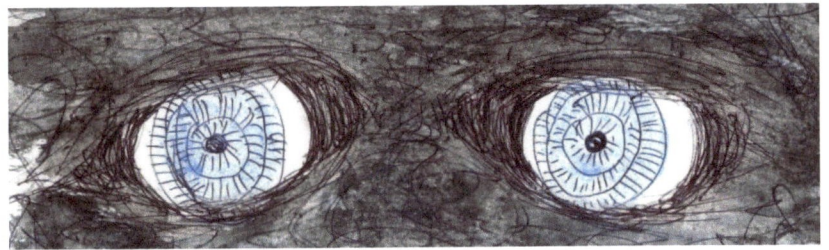

Then she went to the

# small world

with the eyes of her bigness

and looked for the bigness

in the eyes of the others who lived there

to find those who had also

glimpsed the secret.

# Together they traveled
## between the worlds –

drinking red wine and turkish coffee,

building fires in the hearths

so the small beings could gather

and making elixers

for the beings of both worlds

that bring sweet contentment—

and a glimpse of wide seeing

and tenderness together.

 they started feeling

too big or too small,

they took the pungent dark medicine of the shaman

so they would remember the secret.

And together they worked

so that the whole world would finally learn

that we are all

# afterword

THIS STORY was written in a small room at the Dondrub Guest House near the Great Stupa in Boudhanath Nepal. It was August 2016 and I was in a great transition without a home base, not knowing what came next and needing to trust the unknown so I could sense my way to the next shape my life was meant to take. It was a shaky time. As the old self melted away and the new was yet to form, the Tibetan Buddhist nuns who ran the guest house made me warm breakfast and tea, changed the sheets and swept the courtyard, watered the potted plants and the garden. I heard them chant every morning, and in the evenings, I heard through my window the breaking of billiards in the restaurant next door where the Nepalese men gathered after work to relax. "Yes, Boss!" they would exclaim to one another, and laugh off the day in a ritual that repeated as reliably as the nun's daily practices.

Amidst these sounds, the story poured out in one sitting. When I finished writing, I impulsively bought children's watercolors, a black flair pen and a pad of drawing paper. I then spent two days scribbling these drawings. Somehow, they satisfied something in me and I thought to make a little book.

Perhaps the fairytale quality in the story and freedom of the scribbles helped me lighten up about the situation I was in. The story also gave me a clue to the direction I was to take: combining the wide seeing that I learned from the Tibetan Buddhists with a simple, earthy way of life. I had been reading deeply about St. Francis of Assisi, and he seemed such a clear example of one who embodied this that I decided to visit his birthplace in Umbria, Italy, where I found his spirit still very much alive amidst all the red wine and olive trees.

I spent three months soaking up the land where St. Francis lived an imminent spirituality, close to the earth. He praised the sun and moon as brother and sister, saw the divine in the small and the humble, followed intuition and joy, trust and love, and for centuries after, has inspired others just by fully being himself without apology for his flawed and vulnerable humanness.

NOW IT IS JUNE 2017. After the red wine of Italy, the story's prescription of the shaman's pungeant medicine drew me to visit the Shapibo medicine people in the Amazon jungle, something to which I have long been drawn but never before ventured to do. Their embodied wisdom, connection to the spirits of the ancestors, profound knowledge of plants, and mysterious healing songs (called *ikaros*) have provided an ancient medicine that enabled my soul to connect in a new way to body, world and spirit, giving me glimpses of what it means to bring together big and small, vast and human, as St. Francis did. Thanks to the founders, staff, and fellow travelers at the Temple of the Way of Light for the depth of your commitment to the healing of the world. And a deep bow to Maestra Lila and Maestro Damian, who I admire with all my heart, both as masterful healers and as living examples of embodied love and wholeness.

More deep gratitude to Bernhard Karshagen—along with Liza Marie, Rose and Francis—whose magic garden in the Sacred Valley has been a welcoming place to integrate as I slept many nights alone there in the elegant blue light of the moon. Spending time in their garden has been just what I needed to begin embodying what is newly emerging in me. What exactly that is, I can't yet know, except that it involves a shedding of who I thought I was in favor of a trusting, wide-open heart and a fierce commitment to what is real in myself, in others and in the world.

*—Jane Brunette, June 2017*
*Sacred Valley of the Incas, Peru*

# about the author

Jane Brunette *teaches and writes about meditation, spirituality and creating a soulful life in challenging times. She created Writing from the Soul, an approach to writing that has sprouted groups around the world, and she mentors individuals in writing and spiritual practice. Trained as a psychotherapist and Buddhist teacher with a deep affinity for Christian mysticism and indigenous perspectives, she travels widely to challenge her social conditioning, living simply in cultures where this is still possible to free her time and her mind for contemplation and retreat. She is the author of two collections of poetry,* Grasshopper Guru *(2013) and* Cartoon Kali: Poems for Dangerous Times *(2017), both of which emerged from a long cycle of solitary retreat and pilgrimage. Her websites are writingfromthesoul.net and flamingseed.com.*

*Jane with Maestra Lila and Maestro Damian in the Amazon jungle of Peru at the Temple of the Way of Light.*

www.ingramcontent.com/pod-product-compliance
Lightning Source LLC
Chambersburg PA
CBHW041032170626
46815CB00005B/294